WHEN I AM A SISTER

WHEN I AM A SISTER

BY ROBIN BALLARD

GREENWILLOW BOOKS NEW YORK

FOR JASPER

Pen and ink and watercolors were used for the full-color art. The text type is Futura Book. Copyright © 1998 by Robin Ballard. All rights reserved. No part of this book may be reproduced or utilized in any form or by any means, electronic or mechanical, including photocopying, recording, or by any information storage and retrieval system, without permission in writing from the Publisher, Greenwillow Books, a division of William Morrow & Company, Inc., 1350 Avenue of the Americas, New York, NY 10019. http://www.williammorrow.com
Printed in Hong Kong by South China Printing Company (1988) Ltd.   First Edition   10 9 8 7 6 5 4 3 2 1
Library of Congress Cataloging-in-Publication Data
Ballard, Robin. When I am a sister / by Robin Ballard.
    p.   cm.
Summary: Papa tells his daughter what will change and what will stay the same after he and his new wife have a baby.
ISBN 0-688-15397-6 (trade).   ISBN 0-688-15398-4 (lib. bdg.)   [1. Stepfamilies—Fiction.   2. Sisters—Fiction.
3. Babies—Fiction.]   I. Title.   PZ7.B2125Wh   1998   [E]—dc21   97-6326   CIP   AC

Today I am leaving. The summer with
Papa and my stepmother, Kate, is over.
Everything will be different soon.
They are going to have a baby.

I want to know how it will be when I
come back again. So I ask Papa.

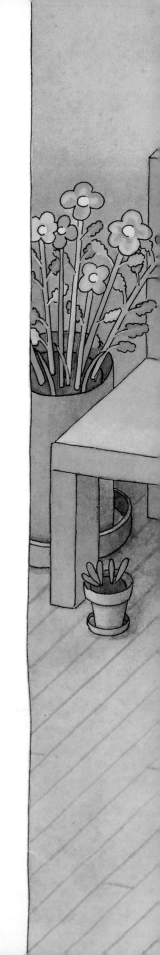

"When I come back, will I still have
my room right next to yours?"

"When you come back," Papa said,
"you will have your own room
downstairs, and we will fix it up
just the way you'd like it to be."

"When I come back, will my things
    still be mine?"

"When you come back," Papa said,
"everything will be waiting here
    for you, just as it always is."

"When I come back, will you and
Kate still read me stories?"

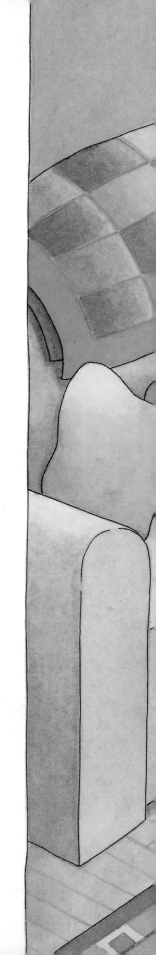

"When you come back," Papa said,
"we will read to you every night,
and you will start to read to us."

"When I come back, will you still
   have the old truck?"

"When you come back," Papa said,
"we will have a bigger truck,
   so there will be room for everyone."

"When I come back, will we still
have our lunches together?"

"When you come back," Papa said,
"you will meet me every Tuesday
for lunch at work."

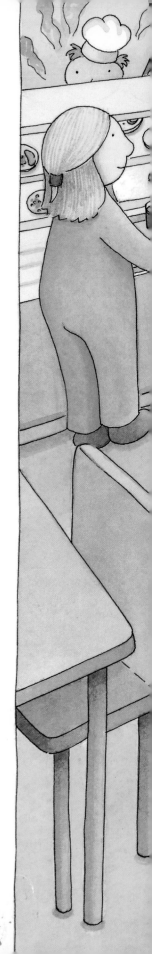

"When I come back, can I still paint
 with Kate in her studio?"

"When you come back," Papa said,
"you will paint your pictures every day
 just as you always do."

"When I come back, will we still
go swimming at the big pool?"

"When you come back," Papa said,
"we will cool off at the pool,
and you can work on your dive."

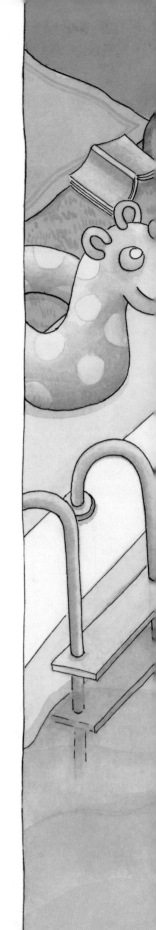

"When I come back, can we still
go to the movies?"

"When you come back," Papa said,
"we will go to the matinee on
Saturday, just you and me together."

"When I come back, I won't be
the only one anymore."

"When you come back," Papa said,
"you will be someone's sister."

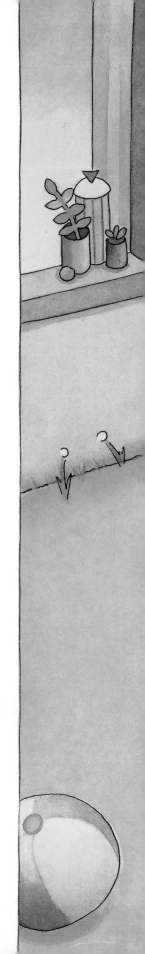

And then it's time for me to go.
We wave and wave good-bye.
Soon I will be with Mama.
I can't wait to see her, and I can't wait
to be a sister when I come back again.

90 Horseneck Road
Montville, N.J. 07045